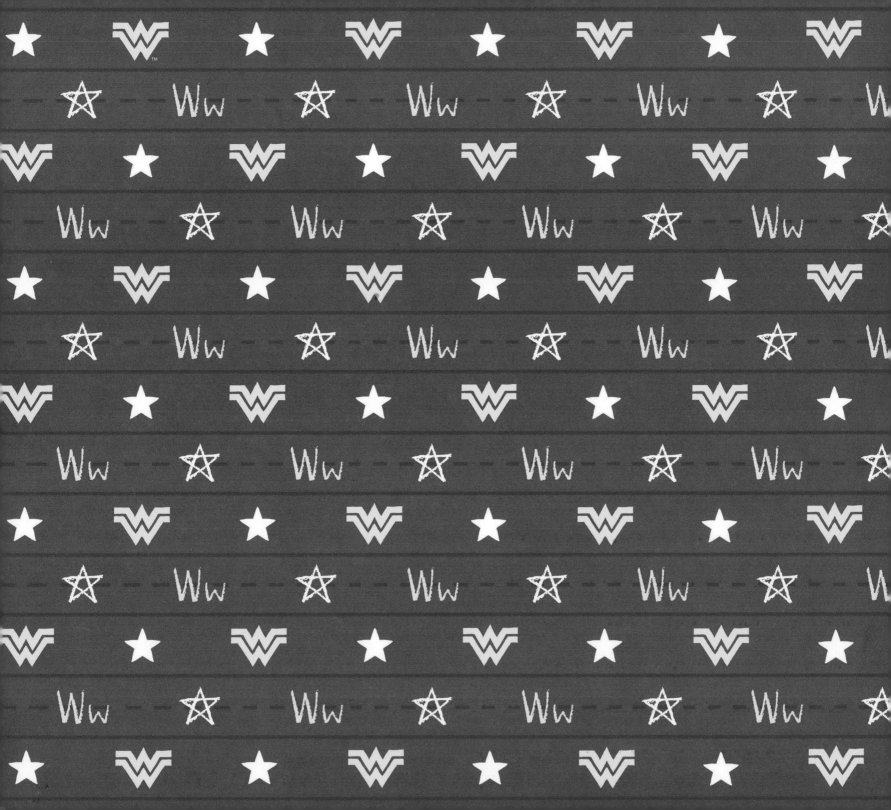

Be a Star, Wonder Woman! is published by
Picture Window Books
a Capstone imprint
1710 Roe Crest Drive
North Mankato, Minnesota 56003
www.mycapstone.com

STAR38959

Cataloging-in-Publication Data is available on the
Library of Congress website.

ISBN: 978-1-5158-1402-3 (hardcover)

Jacket and book design by Bob Lentz

Printed and bound in the USA.
112017   010953R

words by Michael Dahl

pictures by Omar Lozano

BE A STAR,

WONDER WOMAN!

Wonder Woman created by
William Moulton Marston

PICTURE WINDOW BOOKS
a Capstone imprint

New challenges await.

. . . the hero faces each challenge head on.

To restore peace . . .

. . . she must be kind.

Let's play **together** outside instead.

. . . she must
meet alone.

For no matter how tough the challenge . . .

. . . or how difficult the task . . .

. . . a hero must be strong.

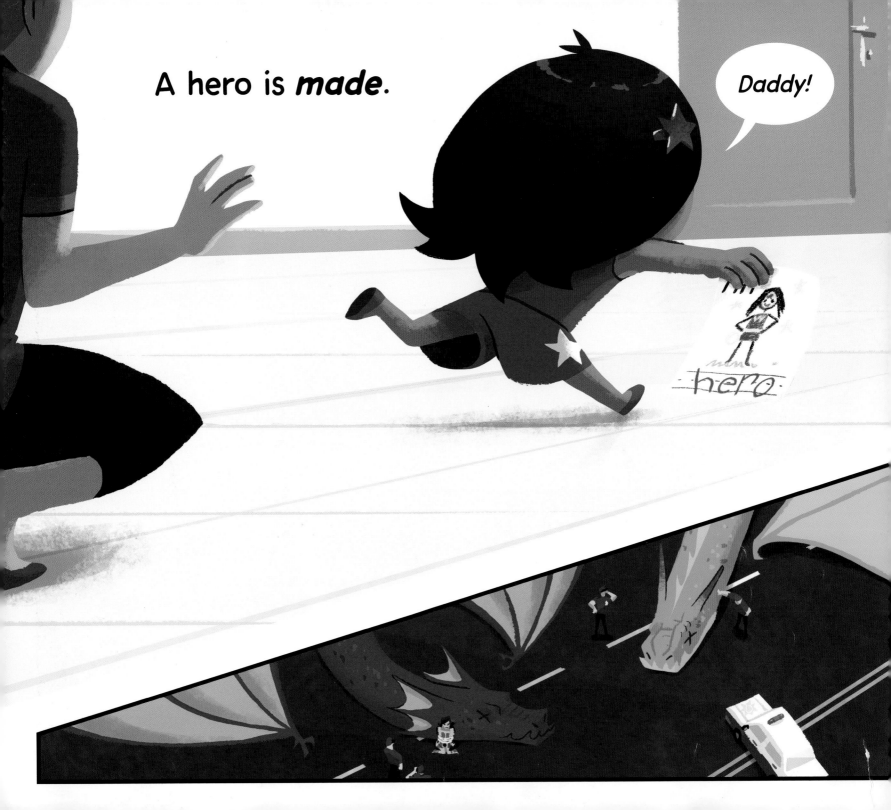

Be a star, Wonder Woman!

Be a STAR Checklist!

Be Prepared

Be Kind

Be Brave

Be Honest

Be Strong

Be Heroic